# Flop the Frog Who Wasn't Quite Right

A book about being **hoppy**...even when you're different.

Written and Illustrated
by
Maurine Frank

*Maurine Frank*

ISBN: 978-1-962935-07-4

Published by High Tide Publications, Inc.
www.hightidepublications.com
Deltaville, Virginia

Thank you for choosing this authorized edition of Flop the Frog Who Wasn't Quite Right – A book about being hoppy...even when you're different.

At High Tide, our mission is to discover, promote, and publish the work of talented authors over 50. Your support by purchasing an authorized copy is crucial in helping us bring their work to you.

Respecting copyright law by refraining from reproducing or scanning any part without our permission is not just about obeying the law, but also about respecting the authors' rights and enabling us to continue supporting them. Your decision to purchase an authorized edition is not only a personal choice, but a valuable contribution to the authors and the entire publishing process. It allows us to bring their work to you and to a wider community of readers.

Your support in our mission to bring the work of our authors to a wider audience is deeply appreciated. Thank you for choosing to purchase an authorized edition.

Edited by Cindy L. Freeman (cindylfreeman.com)

Book design by Firebellied Frog Graphic Design (firebelliedfrog.com)

This book is dedicated to
Edward Montgomery
— a delightful child
who is a bit special
none-the-less courageous
and
adventuresome, loving,
and
willing to take on the best
the world has to offer
— And —
he has
the most delightful smile
you've ever seen!

Hi, Adult!

Embark on an exploratory journey
with a frog and his friends
who have a message
for every special kid.
Flop the frog
shares his problems and insights
in this fun and inspiring story
about finding your personal path.

This book contains encouragement
and activity pages
intended to uplift any kids
who grapple with finding
value in themselves.

Give your kid a hand-up
with this reassuring book!

Hi there, kid!
Do you sometimes have bad days?
This book can help!

Flop the Frog has lots of "HOPPY THOUGHTS."
Each HOPPY THOUGHT gives you a good idea,
a new way of thinking,
and a nice feeling inside.
There are 12 HOPPY THOUGHTS hidden in the story.

Use any bright color
to underline these good thoughts
as you read about Flop and his day.

If a bad day comes along,
you will be able to flip through the book
and
quickly read all the HOPPY THOUGHTS.

These will give you good ideas
on how you can feel better
and
have a fun day no matter what.
Maybe you'll even feel like Hopping!

Flop the frog felt like a flop.
His feet weren't like the other frogs.

Instead, he had teeny tiny feet.

No matter how hard he tried to hop straight, he hopped in circles instead.

He would always wind up back where he started.

Flop Feet

Regular Frog Feet

This made him have lots of grumpy, unhappy days.

One particularly grumpy day as he was hopping in a circle, he met a firefly named Flash. He had big wet tears running down his face.

"What's your problem?" Flop asked.

"Go away!" said Flash.

"I will," said Flop, "but I'll soon come right back. You may as well tell me."

Flash said, "Everyone in my family is very bright, but I'm dim. Dim, dim, dim!"

He blinked his taillight, and there was only the smallest fizzle.

"That's nothing," said Flop. "My feet are so tiny that I only hop in circles. I'm useless and feeling very grumpy."

Flash suggested, since they were both grumpy, they should hang out.

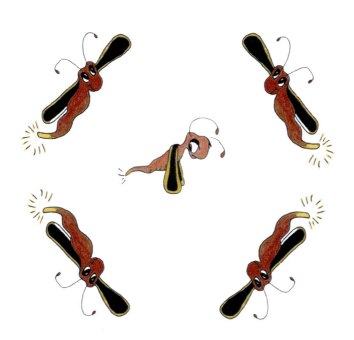

So, off they went, both feeling miserable as they flopped and fizzled along. Suddenly, Flop had a thought. I wonder if it might be hard to feel grumpy when we smile. Maybe we should look for some funny things and see if we feel better.

They saw a brightly colored mushroom, a tree that looked surprised, and a cloud that seemed to be smiling. These sights made them smile too. When they smiled, they felt better. They both realized something. It is impossible to smile and be grumpy at the same time!

Flash said, "I'm not very bright, but I feel better when I am happy. I can decide for myself what to think. I'm going to tell my mind who is boss and think only happy thoughts."

Flop said, "I like that idea. I can only hop in circles. You are not very bright, but it's possible to change how we think about anything at any time!"

Before long, they both giggled and then laughed.

Flop was having so much fun that he began to hop higher and higher until he lost his balance and fell.

KERSPLAT!

Usually when that happened, he'd be reminded of his tiny feet, and he would become grumpy. This time, he decided, "I am going to change how I feel about my problems and make the best of every situation."

Flop looked around while he was on the ground. Sure enough, he found a little rock shaped like a heart. It was a real treasure.

"I have an idea," said Flop. "This heart rock is like a symbol of happiness. Let's throw this happiness rock as far as we can."

"Yes!" said Flash. "We should spread our happiness as far as possible. There could be someone out there who needs to catch it."

Throwing the rock made them feel good. They realized that by making someone else happy, you can make yourself happy!

They laughed some more as they flopped and fizzled along.

Soon they came across an owl sitting all alone.

"Hi!" said Flash who was especially eager to make yet another friend. "I'm Flash. This my friend, Flop. What's your name?"

"Go away!"

Flop said, "We will, but I can only hop in circles, so we'll just come right back. You may as well tell us what is wrong."

"My name is Acree. I'm the worst owl ever! I don't sound like any of the other owls. Listen to me—WHAAT, WHAAT, WHAAAAAT!"

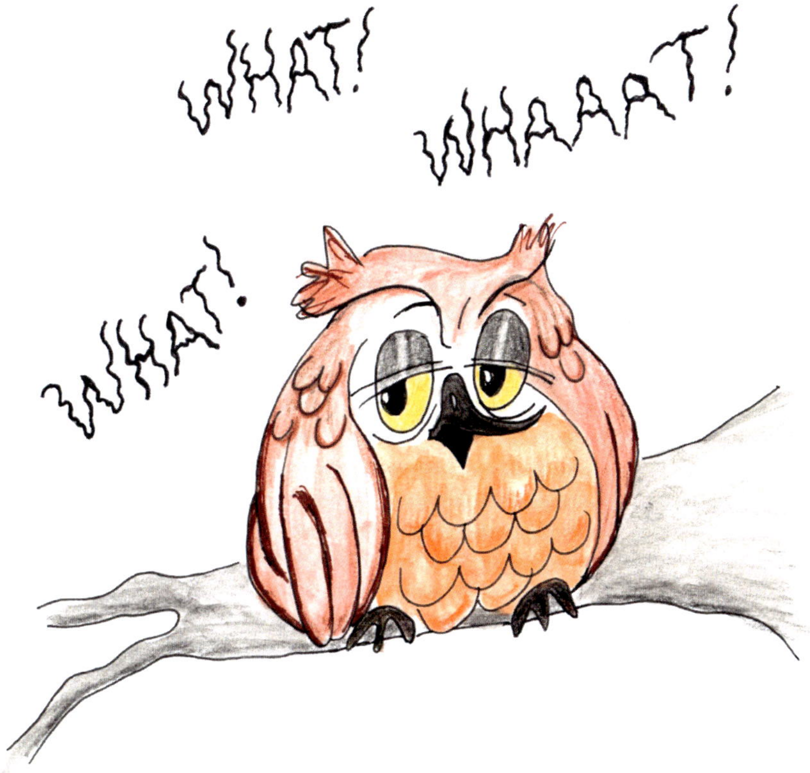
WHAT!
WHAAART!
WHAT!

"Oh my!" said the two new friends.

They had never heard an owl say WHAT instead of WHO but, after all his name was Acree, a very special name which means "free spirit" so who says that an owl has to say WHO? So what if a free spirit wanted to say WHAT.

Flash said, "I think WHAT is an excellent question. WHAT if you decided that saying WHAT is more fun?"

Flop replied, "WHAT if you decided it's okay to be different? WHAT if you decided that being different means being special?"

Acree liked their attitude, so he joined them on their journey. They flopped, fizzled, and what-ed along, each feeling much better.

Flop said, "I can only hop in circles, but it's not our problems that matter; it's what we think about our problems that counts. Instead of worrying about how far I can go, I will just notice how far I have come!"

Flash said, "True. I believe I can get brighter if I keep trying. The only things not possible are the things I don't try to do."

Acree the Owl said, "I think believing in yourself matters most. If I believe that saying WHAT is just as good as saying WHO..." He stopped and looked shocked.

"I just said WHO! I can say WHOOOO! That means nothing is impossible! In fact, the word impossible itself says, 'I'm possible!' Saying WHOO was always possible. I just had to believe in myself!"

"That's right," said Flop. "Going in circles is okay because that means we can never get lost! If our path is a tiny bit different than others', that's okay! It just means..."

"We are special!" they all said together.

We are special!

About that time, they realized they were right back where they had started. They had gone in a great big circle.

"Should we go around once more?" they asked each other.

They started hopping, and sparkling, and WHO-ing around, smiling and laughing, having learned that happiness is always a choice.

Just down the way was a fat, round, grumpy snail. She felt like she must be the fattest, slowest snail ever.

However, on this day a beautiful heart rock had dropped out of the sky right in front of her. She was very surprised!

"I wonder where this special rock came from?" she thought, as she slowly poked along—but now with a big smile on her face.

The End

PS — Don't forget to go back and underline all the HOPPY THOUGHTS you can find. There are 12.

Any time you are having a grumpy day, read Flop's HOPPY THOUGHTS that you've marked, and he promises that you will feel better! You might go from grumpy to "hoppy" (even if you go in circles)!

And if you do, it's okay so long as you have a big smile on your face because...remember...

You can't be grumpy and smile at the same time.

# About the Author

Children's book author Maurine Frank believes that every individual is significant. Children, in particular, have a special light that needs to be developed, encouraged, and uplifted.

*Flop the Frog Who Wasn't Quite Right* is her third book that focuses on enhancing that light—especially for kids who don't fit in, feel discouraged, or struggle with self-esteem and confidence.

The book is a result of years of training in personal development, team effectiveness, and inner growth—scaled to a child's understanding with Hoppy Thoughts— positive affirmations that inspire ideas for good days, even on a bad day. She writes books of love for kids trying to find their way through a difficult world.

## Did you find all the Hoppy Thoughts? If not, here they are:

1. It is impossible to smile and be grumpy at the same time!

2. I'm going to tell my mind who is boss and think only happy thoughts!

3. It's possible to change how we think about anything at any time!

4. I am going to change how I feel about my problems and make the best of every situation.

5. By making someone else happy, you can make yourself happy!

6. WHAT if you decided it's okay to be different?
   WHAT if you decided that being different means being special!

7.   It's not our problems that matter; it's what we think about our problems that counts.

8.   The only things not possible are the things I don't try to do.

9.   I think believing in yourself matters most.

10.  Nothing is impossible! In fact, the word impossible itself says "I'm possible!"

11.  If our path is a tiny bit different than others', that's okay! It just means we are special.

12.  Happiness is always a choice.

# Other Books by Maurine Frank

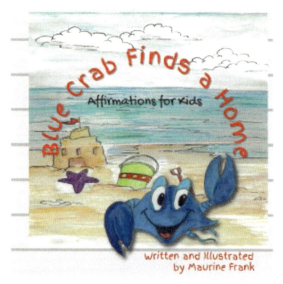

About Blue Crab Finds a Home

I know that every individual is significant and believe that our existence affects countless people in countless ways. I also believe that within each of us is a spark that can be extinguished or can glow based on encouragement from others. I'm convinced that taking pride in our light and using it for good is essential and it begins at an early age.

Lilly was a ladybug who loved to snuggle in her little burrow under a beautiful leaf that had a very unusual shape. It wrapped around her perfectly.

One day a storm and rain washed over the bank, down the furrows, and into her little burrow. Her wonderful leaf blanket floated away. She was sad. Her leaf blanket was extraordinary; she had never seen another like it.

Join Lilly as she searches for a new leaf with help from her tree friends. This delightful book by author and artist Maurine Frank entertains and teaches young readers about trees through her beautiful illustrations and hands-on activities.

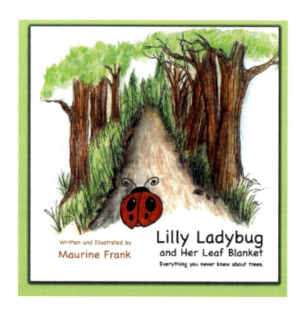

# If you enjoyed this book...

## Please leave a review on Amazon.

Here are some instructions:

1. Watch this video:
   https://www.youtube.com/watch?app=desktop&v=eYyFoMWTEns&t=6

2. Or follow these instructions:

To leave a book review on Amazon, you can:
- Go to the product detail page for the book
- Select Write a product review in the Customer Reviews section
- Choose a star rating
- Add text, photos, or videos
- Select Submit

You can also leave a review by going to Your Orders if you've placed an order for the book.

Amazon has certain eligibility requirements for posting reviews:
- You must have spent at least $50 on Amazon in the last 12 months
- Your review must follow Amazon's Community Guidelines

Made in the USA
Middletown, DE
26 November 2024

65479538R00027